Iluvaetarus

Hc est dracones

Mons
Solus

Lacus
Longus

Silva
Obscurus

Rivendellus

Oppidum
Hobbitorum

Flumine
Brandyvinum

Flumine
Magno

Inundatio Griseus

Montes Nebulosi

Silva
Fangornus

Latibulo terrae incolabat
hobbitus. Nec rancidulum
sordidum humidumque
latibulum, nec caudae
vermorum atque odore
limi plenum.

Gaendalfus Magus Canus

Bilbo greets Gandalf with smoke rings.

Bilbo Gaendalfum salute dicebat cum coronas fumos.

Dumili ad latibulo Bilbonis adveniant.

Dwarves arrive at Bilbo's hobbit hole.

A rowdy and unexpected dinner party.

Convivium rusticum inopinatumque.

Gaendalfus tabulam geographicam Throrem clavemque ad Thorino dabat.

Gandalf gives Thror's map and key to Thorin

Thorinus Rex sub Monte

The company passes through the lonely lands and make camp in the rain.

Sodalitas per desolatis~terris permeant et castram in pluvia constituant.

The company searching out a light in the forest come across three trolls.

The dwarves are captured by the trolls until the monsters are turned into stone.

Sodalitas ad lucem investigus tres troglodytes invenieant. Pumili a troglodytes captivitantur dum monsteri lapides vertantur.

The company arriues at Riuendell' where Elrond dwells in the last homely house.

Sodalitas a Rivendello perveniabant qua Elrond in domi familiaris habitabat.

Elrond reueals the name of Gandalf's sword

Elrond nomen gladii Gaendalfi revelat.

Elrond litterae lunae in tabula geographica revelat.

Elrond reueals the moon letters on the map.

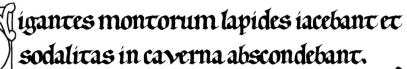

Gigantes montorum lapides iacebant et sodalitas in caverna abscondebant.

Sodalitas a gobelini capti ad Gobelino Magno exhibentur. Gaendalfus perveniat et gobelines dispergat.

Bilbo discouers a ring in the passage way.

In traductum Bilbo anulum inueniat.

 enigmata in tenebris cum Gollo.

Riddles in the dark with Gollum.

Bilbo is inuisible, and escapes from Gollum and the goblins.

 ilbo inuisibilis est, et gobelinibus Golloque ecfugiat.

Aenigmata

Exiguum corposi munus mucronis adunci
Fallacis escas medio circumfero fluctu
Blandior, ut noceam; morti praemitto saginas.

My form is small, the crooked dagger's pride, With treacherous lures, throughout
the stream I hide; I charm to hurt, and then my food to death confide.

Longa sed exilis, tenui producta metallo,
Mollia duco levi comitantia vincula ferro,
Et faciem laesis et nexum redo solutis.

Long and thin am I, of metal slight, My yielding chain I draw by iron light,
I shape the torn and bind the loosened tight.

Dentibus innumeris sum toto corpore plena,
Frondicomas suboles morsu depascor acuto,
Mando tamen frustra, quod respuo praemia
dentis.

By countless teeth is all my body lined, The forest's sons I fell with bite
unkind, And yet in vain I eat, I throw it all behind.

Saepta gravi ferro, levibus circumdata pinnis
Aera per medium volucri contendo meatu,
Missaque descendens nullo mittente revertor.

With heavy iron bound and feathers light, Through middle of the air I hold
my rapid flight, Sent upward I return without a sender's might.

The
company
flees from
the wargs
and goblins
and climbs
into the
trees.

odalitas a gobelinibus wargibusque
fugiant et arbores scandant.

In the
tree
Gandalf
hurls
flaming
pinecones
at the
wargs.

In arbore Gaendal-
fus pineas ardens
iaciat ad wargibus.

quilae veniant
et sodalitatem
salvant.

The
eagles
come and
rescue the
company.

The
company
arriues
at the
house of
Beorn.

Sodalitas perve-
niant a domo
Beorni.

Beorn gigans
apiariusque
est.

Beorn is
a giant
and a
beekeeper.

Beorn
offers
hospitality
to the
company
and hears
their tale.

Beorn ad sodalitati
hospitium offerat
et audiat fabulum eorum.

Ursus magnus ad
porta scalpturiat.

A large
bear
scratches
at the
door.

The company wanders and becomes lost in Mirkwood Forest.

In Silvam Obscurum sodalitas errant.

Araneae ingentes morsum Aculei sentient.

The giant spiders feel the bite of Sting.

Bilbo frees the dwarves from the web traps of the spiders.

Bilbo liberat pumilos a textibus aranearum.

Sed Thorinum pumilosque captivae factae sunt per dryadali.

But Thorin and the dwarves are taken prisoner by the wood elves.

The dwarues
are held
captiue in
the dungeons
of the
Eluen-
King. Bilbo
obserues the
wood-elues
who are
drunk.

Pumili captivos sunt in carcerem Regis-
dryadum. Bilbo conspiciat dryados-
silvestrios qui temulentus sunt.

The
dwarues
escape in
barrels.

In cupas pumili
abscondant.

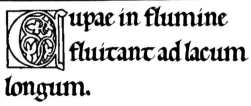

Cupae in flumine
fluitant ad lacum
longum.

The
barrels
float doun
the riuer
touards
the Long
Lake.

The
dwarves
are
released
from the
barrels.

 umili a cupis
eximuntur.

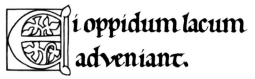 i oppidum lacum
adveniant.

Thorin is
presented
to the
Master of
Lake
Town.

 horinus ad
Magistrem
praesentur.

 avigant ad
Montem Solum.

The
company
sails on
to the
Lonely
Mountain.

odalitas ad Montem Solum preuenient usque ianuam occultam inuenire possunt.

n diem Durinum ianuae reuelatus est per luminem lunam.

The burglar descends the passage into the caverns where the dragon sleeps.

Affractarius in cavernam descendat ubi draco dormit.

Bilbo is invisible and converses with Smaug.

Bilbo invisibilis est, et cum Smaugum colloquit.

Iratus draco ex monte volat, et sodalitas in cavernis obsaepto est.

The furious dragon flies out of the mountain and the company is trapped inside.

De draconibus. Draco maior cunctorum serpentium sive animantium omnium super terram. hinc Greci dracon ta vocant, unde et dirivatum est in Latinum; ut draco diceretur. Qui serpe ab speluncis abstractus fertur in aerem, concitaturque propter eum aer. Est autem cristatus, ore parvo, et artis fistulis per quas trahit spiritum et linguam exerat. Vim autem non in dentibus set in cauda habet, et verbere pocius quam ictu nocet. Innoxius tamen a venenis. Sed ideo huic ad mortem faciendam venena non esse necessaria dicunt, quia siquem ligaverit occidit. A quo nec elephans tutus est sui corporis magnitudine. Nam circa semitas delitescens, per quas elephantes soliti gradiuntur crura eorū nodis illigat, ac suffocatos perimit. Gignitur autem in Ethiopia et India, estus. huic draimmanissim⁹ concitatur, imis se et decipit

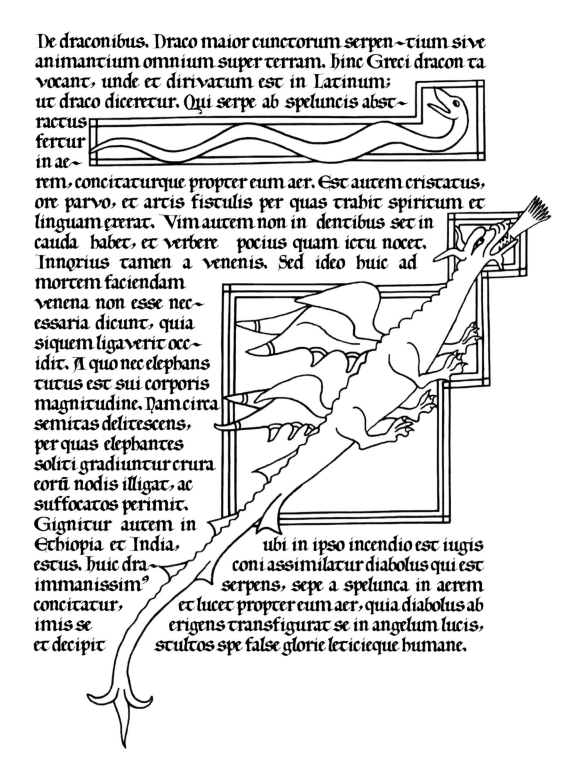

ubi in ipso incendio est iugis coni assimilatur diabolus qui est serpens, sepe a spelunca in aerem et lucet propter eum aer, quia diabolus ab erigens transfigurat se in angelum lucis, stultos spe false glorie leticieque humane.

The dwarues recouer the treasure while the dragon is gone.

Pumili thesaurum recuperant dum draco absens est.

The company seeks out the riuer gate.

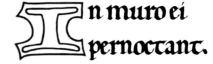 Sodalitas exitum flumen vestigant.

In muro ei pernoctant.

They spend the night on the walls.

Smaug appugnat
oppidum lacum.

Bardus sagittam
nigram ad Smau~
gum sagittat.

The
dwarues
recouer the
treasure
while the
dragon is
gone.

The
townsfolk
acclaim
Bard to
make him
king.

Oppidani Bardū
regem facere
probant.

Milites et homines
armati ad Montem
Solum progredient.

Soldiers
and men
at-arms
march to
the Lonely
Mountain.

Bardus de Oppidum Lacum

The dwarues repair the ruined battlements.

Pumili murum pruinosum reparant.

Socii dryadali hominesque ad Montem Solum adveniant.

The eluish and human allies arriue at the Lonely Mountain.

Bard and the Elf King demand that the treasure be diuided up among them. Thorin refuses.

ardus Rex ~ dryadumque partitione thesauri postulant. Thorinus recusat.

Bilbo climbs down from the wall in the night.

Bilbo de muro descendat in nocte.

Arkenlapide ad Bardum datum est cum Rege~dryadus.

The Arkenstone is given to Bard with the Eluen King.

Gandalf bids good-bye while Bilbo returns to the wall.

Gaendalfus valedicat dum Bilbo ad murum redeat.

Bardus Arkenlapidum osten dant a Thorino.

Dainus adveniat a Colle Ferro et socies provocat.

Gobelini wargique adveniant, et Gaendalfus praemonitium dabat.

Bilbo awakens on the battlefield.

Bilbo in campus surgit.

Thorinus morior dum amici valedicant.

Thorin lies dying while his friends bid him farewell.

The elves and men of Lake Town divide the treasure and return home.

Dryadali hominesque thesaurum partitiant.

Beornus vale dicit ad Gaendalfum Bilbonemque.

Beorn bids farewell to Gandalf and Bilbo.

Gandalf and Bilbo bid farewell to Elrond.

Gaendalfus Bilboque ad Elrondum valedicant.

The trolls' treasure is recouered.

 hesaurum troglody-torũ recuperatur.

 ilbo ad oppidũ hobbitorum reveniat.

Bilbo returns to Hobbiton.

Made in the USA
Coppell, TX
18 January 2020